W9-ADN-444

disc

ALL ABOARD!

PASSENGER TRAINS

Phillip Ryan

PowerKiDS press™

New York

Published in 2011 by The Rosen Publishing Group, Inc.
29 East 21st Street, New York, NY 10010

Copyright © 2011 by The Rosen Publishing Group, Inc.

All rights reserved. No part of this book may be reproduced in any form without permission in writing from the publisher, except by a reviewer.

First Edition

Editor: Joanne Randolph
Book Design: Ashley Burrell
Photo Researcher: Jessica Gerweck

Photo Credits: Cover © Gavriel Jecan/age fotostock; p. 5 © Mark Turner/age fotostock; pp. 6–7, 9, 10–11, 14–15, 18–19 Shutterstock.com; p. 13 © Javier Larrea/age fotostock; p. 17 Bob Thomas/Getty Images; p. 21 Andrew Holt/Getty Images; p. 22–23 www.iStockphoto.com/Judy Barranco.

Library of Congress Cataloging-in-Publication Data
Ryan, Phillip.
  Passenger trains / by Phillip Ryan. — 1st ed.
      p. cm. — (All aboard!)
  Includes index.
  ISBN 978-1-4488-0637-9 (library binding) — ISBN 978-1-4488-1215-8 (pbk.) —
ISBN 978-1-4488-1216-5 (6-pack)
  1. Railroad trains—Juvenile literature. 2. Passenger trains—Juvenile literature. 3. Railroad passenger cars—Juvenile literature. I. Title.
  TF148.R937 2011
  385'.22—dc22
                              2009049059
Manufactured in the United States of America

PSIA Compliance Information: Batch #WS10PK: For Further Information contact Rosen Publishing, New York, New York at 1-800-237-9932

R0430443363

CONTENTS

Here comes a **passenger** train! Passenger trains carry people.

Passenger trains run on tracks. The tracks can be straight or they can bend.

6

Passenger trains are made up of cars. The first car is the **engine**. It pulls the train.

People wait for the train at the station. They stand on a **platform** to wait.

Inside the train there are seats where you can sit. You might get to sit by a **window**.

Passenger trains carry people into and out of cities, too.

Japan has a fast passenger train called a bullet train. It gets its name from its shape.

There are fast passenger trains in many countries. This one carries people in France.

Going to a new place on a passenger train can be fun. Where would you want to go?

22

WORDS TO KNOW

engine

 passenger

platform

 window

INDEX

WEB SITES

Due to the changing nature of Internet links, PowerKids Press has developed an online list of Web sites related to the subject of this book. This site is updated regularly. Please use this link to access the list: www.powerkidslinks.com/allabrd/pt/